THE FOOL OF THE WORLD AND THE FLYING SHIP

A Russian Tale

THE FOOL OF THE WORLD
AND THE FLYING SHIP

 Retold by ARTHUR RANSOME | Pictures by URI SHULEVITZ

A SUNBURST BOOK

FARRAR, STRAUS AND GIROUX

There were once upon a time an old peasant and his wife, and they had three sons. Two of them were clever young men who could borrow money without being cheated, but the third was the Fool of the World. He was as simple as a child, simpler than some children, and he never did anyone a harm in his life.

Well, it always happens like that. The father and mother thought a lot of the two smart young men; but the Fool of the World was lucky if he got enough to eat, because they always forgot him unless they happened to be looking at him, and sometimes even then.

But however it was with his father and mother, this is a story that shows that God loves simple folk, and turns things to their advantage in the end.

For it happened that the Czar of that country sent out messengers along the highroads and the rivers, even to huts in the forest like ours, to say that he would give his daughter, the Princess, in marriage to anyone who could bring him a flying ship—ay, a ship with wings, that should sail this way and that through the blue sky, like a ship sailing on the sea.

"This is a chance for us," said the two clever brothers; and that same day they set off together, to see if one of them could not build the flying ship and marry the Czar's daughter, and so be a great man indeed.

And their father blessed them, and gave them finer

clothes than ever he wore himself. And their mother made them up hampers of food for the road, soft white rolls, and several kinds of cooked meats, and bottles of corn brandy. She went with them as far as the highroad, and waved her hand to them till they were out of sight. And so the two clever brothers set merrily off on their adventure, to see what could be done with their cleverness. And what happened to them I do not know, for they were never heard of again.

The Fool of the World saw them set off, with their fine parcels of food, and their fine clothes, and their bottles of corn brandy.

"I'd like to go too," says he, "and eat good meat, with soft white rolls, and drink corn brandy, and marry the Czar's daughter."

"Stupid fellow," says his mother, "what's the good of your going? Why, if you were to stir from the house you would walk into the arms of a bear; and if not that, then the wolves would eat you before you had finished staring at them."

But the Fool of the World would not be held back by words. "I am going," says he. "I am going. I am going. I am going."

He went on saying this over and over again, till the old woman, his mother, saw there was nothing to be done, and was glad to get him out of the house so as to be quit of the sound of his voice. So she put some food in a bag for him to eat by the way. She put in the bag some crusts of dry black bread and a flask of water. She did not even bother to go as far as the footpath to see him on his way. She saw the last of him at the door of the hut, and he had not taken two steps before she had gone back into the hut to see to more important business.

No matter. The Fool of the World set off with his bag over his shoulder, singing as he went, for he was off to seek his fortune and marry the Czar's daughter. He was sorry his mother had not given him any corn brandy; but he sang merrily for all that. He would have liked white rolls instead of the dry black crusts; but, after all, the main thing on a journey is to have something to eat. So he trudged

merrily along the road, and sang because the trees were
green and there was a blue sky overhead.

He had not gone very far when he met an ancient old
man with a bent back, and a long beard, and eyes hidden
under his bushy eyebrows.

"Good day, young fellow," says the ancient old man.

"Good day, grandfather," says the Fool of the World.

"And where are you off to?" says the ancient old man.

"What!" says the Fool. "Haven't you heard? The Czar is going to give his daughter to anyone who can bring him a flying ship."

"And you can really make a flying ship?" says the ancient old man.

"No, I do not know how."

"Then what are you going to do?"

"God knows," says the Fool of the World.

"Well," says the ancient, "if things are like that, sit you down here. We will rest together and have a bite of food. Bring out what you have in your bag."

"I am ashamed to offer you what I have here. It is good enough for me, but it is not the sort of meal to which one can ask guests."

"Never mind that. Out with it. Let us eat what God has given."

The Fool of the World opened his bag, and could hardly believe his eyes. Instead of black crusts he saw fresh white rolls and cooked meats. He handed them out to the ancient, who said, "You see how God loves simple folk. Although your own mother does not love you, you have not been done out of your share of the good things. Let's have a sip at the corn brandy. . . ."

The Fool of the World opened his flask, and instead of water there came out corn brandy, and that of the best. So the Fool and the ancient made merry, eating and drinking; and when they had done, and sung a song or two together, the ancient says to the Fool:

"Listen to me. Off with you into the forest. Go up to the first big tree you see. Make the sacred sign of the cross three times before it. Strike it a blow with your little hatchet. Fall backwards on the ground, and lie there, full length on your back, until somebody wakes you up. Then you will find the ship made, all ready to fly. Sit you down in it, and fly off whither you want to go. But be sure on the way to give a lift to everyone you meet."

The Fool of the World thanked the ancient old man, said goodbye to him, and went off to the forest. He walked up to a tree, the first big tree he saw, made the sign of the cross three times before it, swung his hatchet round his neck, struck a mighty blow on the trunk of the tree, instantly fell backwards flat on the ground, closed his eyes, and went to sleep.

A little time went by, and it seemed to the Fool as he slept that somebody was jogging his elbow. He woke up and opened his eyes. His hatchet, worn out, lay beside him. The big tree was gone, and in its place there stood a little ship, ready and finished. The Fool did not stop to think. He jumped into the ship, seized the tiller, and sat down. Instantly the ship leapt up into the air and sailed away over the tops of the trees.

The little ship answered the tiller as readily as if she were sailing in water, and the Fool steered for the highroad, and sailed along above it, for he was afraid of losing his way if he tried to steer a course across the open country.

He flew on and on, and looked down, and saw a man lying in the road below him with his ear on the damp ground.

"Good day to you, uncle," cried the Fool.

"Good day to you, Sky-fellow," cried the man.

"What are you doing down there?" says the Fool.

"I am listening to all that is being done in the world."

"Take your place in the ship with me."

The man was willing enough, and sat down in the ship with the Fool, and they flew on together singing songs.

They flew on and on, and looked down, and there was a man on one leg, with the other tied up to his head.

"Good day, uncle," says the Fool, bringing the ship to the ground. "Why are you hopping along on one foot?"

"If I were to untie the other I should move too fast. I should be stepping across the world in a single stride."

"Sit down with us," says the Fool.

The man sat down with them in the ship, and they flew on together singing songs.

They flew on and on, and looked down, and there was
a man with a gun, and he was taking aim, but what he was
aiming at they could not see.

"Good health to you, uncle," says the Fool. "But what
are you shooting at? There isn't a bird to be seen."

"What!" says the man. "If there were a bird that you
could see, I should not shoot at it. A bird or a beast a thou-
sand versts away, that's the sort of mark for me."

"Take your seat with us," says the Fool.

The man sat down with them in the ship, and they flew
on together. Louder and louder rose their songs.

They flew on and on, and looked down, and there was a man carrying a sack full of bread on his back.

"Good health to you, uncle," says the Fool, sailing down. "And where are you off to?"

"I am going to get bread for my dinner."

"But you've got a full sack on your back."

"That—that little scrap! Why, that's not enough for a single mouthful."

"Take your seat with us," says the Fool.

The Eater sat down with them in the ship, and they flew on together, singing louder than ever.

They flew on and on, and looked down, and there was a man walking round and round a lake.

"Good health to you, uncle," says the Fool. "What are you looking for?"

"I want a drink, and I can't find any water."

"But there's a whole lake in front of your eyes. Why can't you take a drink from that?"

"That little drop!" says the man. "Why, there's not enough water there to wet the back of my throat if I were to drink it at one gulp."

"Take your seat with us," says the Fool.

The Drinker sat down with them, and again they flew on, singing in chorus.

They flew on and on, and looked down, and there was a man walking towards the forest, with a fagot of wood on his shoulders.

"Good day to you, uncle," says the Fool. "Why are you taking wood to the forest?"

"This isn't simple wood," says the man.

"What is it, then?" says the Fool.

"If it is scattered about, a whole army of soldiers leaps out of the ground."

"There's a place for you with us," says the Fool.

The man sat down with them, and the ship rose up into the air, and flew on, carrying its singing crew.

They flew on and on, and looked down, and there was
a man carrying a sack of straw.

"Good health to you, uncle," says the Fool. "And where
are you taking your straw?"

"To the village."

"Why, are they short of straw in your village?"

"No; but this is such straw that if you scatter it abroad
in the very hottest of the summer, instantly the weather

turns colder, and there is snow and frost.''

''There's a place here for you too,'' says the Fool.

''Very kind of you,'' says the man, and steps in and sits down, and away they all sail together, singing like to burst their lungs.

They did not meet anyone else, and presently came flying up to the palace of the Czar. They flew down and cast anchor in the courtyard.

Just then the Czar was eating his dinner. He heard their loud singing and looked out of the window and saw the ship come sailing down into his courtyard. He sent his servant out to ask who was the great prince who had brought him the flying ship and had come sailing down with such a merry noise of singing.

The servant came up to the ship and saw the Fool of the World and his companions sitting there cracking jokes. He saw they were all moujiks, simple peasants, sitting in the ship; so he did not stop to ask questions, but came back quietly and told the Czar that there were no gentlemen in the ship at all, but only a lot of dirty peasants.

Now the Czar was not at all pleased with the idea of giving his only daughter in marriage to a simple peasant, and he began to think how he could get out of his bargain. Thinks he to himself, "I'll set them such tasks that they will not be able to perform, and they'll be glad to get off with their lives, and I shall get the ship for nothing."

So he told his servant to go to the Fool and tell him that before the Czar had finished his dinner the Fool was to bring him some of the magical water of life.

Now, while the Czar was giving this order to his servant, the Listener, the first of the Fool's companions, was listening and heard the words of the Czar and repeated them to the Fool.

"What am I to do now?" says the Fool, stopping short in his jokes. "In a year, in a whole century, I never could find that water. And he wants it before he has finished his dinner."

"Don't you worry about that," says the Swift-goer, "I'll deal with that for you."

The servant came and announced the Czar's command.

"Tell him he will have it," says the Fool.

His companion, the Swift-goer, untied his foot from beside his head, put it to the ground, wriggled it a little to get the stiffness out of it, ran off, and was out of sight almost before he had stepped from the ship. Quicker than I can tell it you in words, he had come to the water of life and put some of it in a bottle.

"I shall have plenty of time to get back," thinks he, and down he sits under a windmill and goes off to sleep.

The royal dinner was coming to an end, and there wasn't a sign of him. There were no songs and no jokes in the flying ship. Everybody was watching for the Swift-goer and thinking he would not be in time.

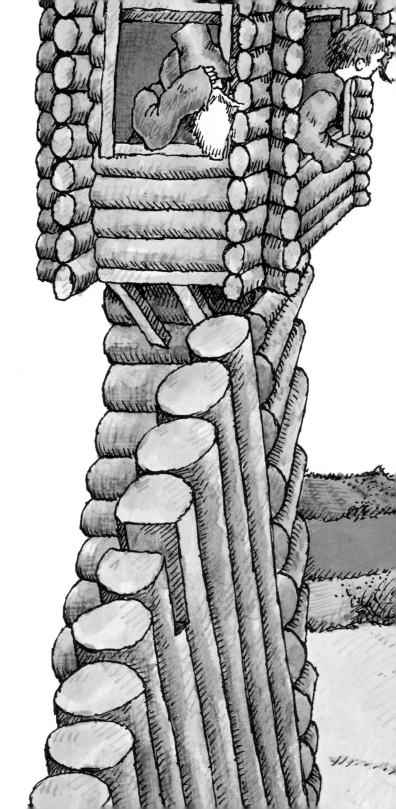

The Listener jumped out and laid his right ear to the damp ground, listened a moment, and said, "What a fellow! He has gone to sleep under the windmill. I can hear him snoring. And there is a fly buzzing with its wings, perched on the windmill close above his head."

"This is my affair," says the Far-shooter, and he picked up his gun from between his knees, aimed at the fly on the

windmill, and woke the Swift-goer with the thud of the bullet on the wood of the mill close by his head. The Swift-goer leapt up and ran, and in less than a second had brought the magic water of life and given it to the Fool. The Fool gave it to the servant, who took it to the Czar. The Czar had not yet left the table, so that his command had been fulfilled as exactly as ever could be.

"What fellows these peasants are," thought the Czar. "There is nothing for it but to set them another task." So the Czar said to his servant, "Go to the captain of the flying ship and give him this message: 'If you are such a cunning fellow, you must have a good appetite. Let you and your companions eat at a single meal twelve oxen roasted whole, and as much bread as can be baked in forty ovens!'"

The Listener heard the message, and told the Fool what was coming. The Fool was terrified, and said, "I can't get through even a single loaf at a sitting."

"Don't worry about that," said the Eater. "It won't be more than a mouthful for me, and I shall be glad to have a little snack in place of my dinner."

The servant came and announced the Czar's command.

"Good," says the Fool. "Send the food along, and we'll know what to do with it."

So they brought twelve oxen roasted whole, and as much bread as could be baked in forty ovens, and the companions had scarcely sat down to the meal before the Eater had finished the lot.

"Why," said the Eater, "what a little! They might have given us a decent meal while they were about it."

The Czar told his servant to tell the Fool that he and his companions were to drink forty barrels of wine, with forty bucketfuls in every barrel.

The Listener told the Fool what message was coming.

"Why," says the Fool, "I never in my life drank more than one bucket at a time."

"Don't worry," says the Drinker. "You forget that I am thirsty. It'll be nothing of a drink for me."

They brought the forty barrels of wine, and tapped them, and the Drinker tossed them down one after another, one gulp for each barrel. "Little enough," says he. "Why, I am thirsty still."

"Very good," says the Czar to his servant, when he heard that they had eaten all the food and drunk all the wine. "Tell the fellow to get ready for the wedding, and let him go and bathe himself in the bathhouse. But let the bathhouse be made so hot that the man will stifle and frizzle as soon as he sets foot inside. It is an iron bathhouse. Let it be made red-hot."

The Listener heard all this and told the Fool, who stopped short with his mouth open in the middle of a joke.

"Don't you worry," says the moujik with the straw.

Well, they made the bathhouse red-hot, and called the Fool, and the Fool went along to the bathhouse to wash himself, and with him went the moujik with the straw.

They shut them both in the bathhouse and thought that that was the end of them. But the moujik scattered his straw before them as they went in, and it became so cold in there that the Fool of the World had scarcely time to wash himself before the water in the caldrons froze to solid ice. They lay down on the very stove itself, and spent the night there, shivering.

In the morning the servants opened the bathhouse, and there were the Fool of the World and the moujik, alive and well, lying on the stove and singing songs.

They told the Czar, and the Czar raged with anger. "There is no getting rid of this fellow," says he. "But go and tell him that I send him this message: 'If you are to marry my daughter, you must show that you are able to defend her. Let me see that you have at least a regiment of soldiers.'" Thinks he to himself, "How can a simple peasant raise a troop? He will find it hard enough to raise a single soldier."

The Listener told the Fool of the World, and the Fool began to lament. "This time," says he, "I am done indeed. You, my brothers, have saved me from misfortune more than once, but this time, alas, there is nothing to be done."

"Oh, what a fellow you are!" says the peasant with the fagot of wood. "I suppose you've forgotten about me. Remember that I am the man for this little affair, and don't you worry about it at all."

The Czar's servant came along and gave his message.

"Very good," says the Fool. "But tell the Czar that if after this he puts me off again, I'll make war on his country and take the Princess by force."

And then, as the servant went back with the message, the whole crew of the flying ship set to their singing again, and sang and laughed and made jokes as if they had not a care in the world.

During the night, while the others slept, the peasant with the fagot of wood went hither and thither, scattering his sticks. Instantly where they fell there appeared a gigantic army. Nobody could count the number of soldiers in it— cavalry, foot soldiers, yes, and guns, and all the guns new and bright, and the men in the finest uniforms that ever were seen.

In the morning, as the Czar woke and looked from the

windows of the palace, he found himself surrounded by
troops upon troops of soldiers, and generals in cocked hats
bowing in the courtyard and taking orders from the Fool
of the World, who sat there joking with his companions
in the flying ship. Now it was the Czar's turn to be afraid.
As quickly as he could, he sent his servants to the Fool with
presents of rich jewels and fine clothes, invited him to come
to the palace, and begged him to marry the Princess.

The Fool of the World put on the fine clothes and stood there as handsome a young man as a princess could wish for a husband. He presented himself before the Czar, fell in love with the Princess and she with him, married her the

same day, received with her a rich dowry, and became so clever that all the court repeated everything he said. The Czar and the Czaritza liked him very much, and as for the Princess, she loved him to distraction.